AF596080

Belongs to:

COLOR TEST

Feel free to draw and
color anything you want

Turkey Maze

♣ "What key has legs and can't open a door?"
♣ "a turkey."

FEEL FREE TO DRAW AND
COLOR ANYTHING YOU WANT

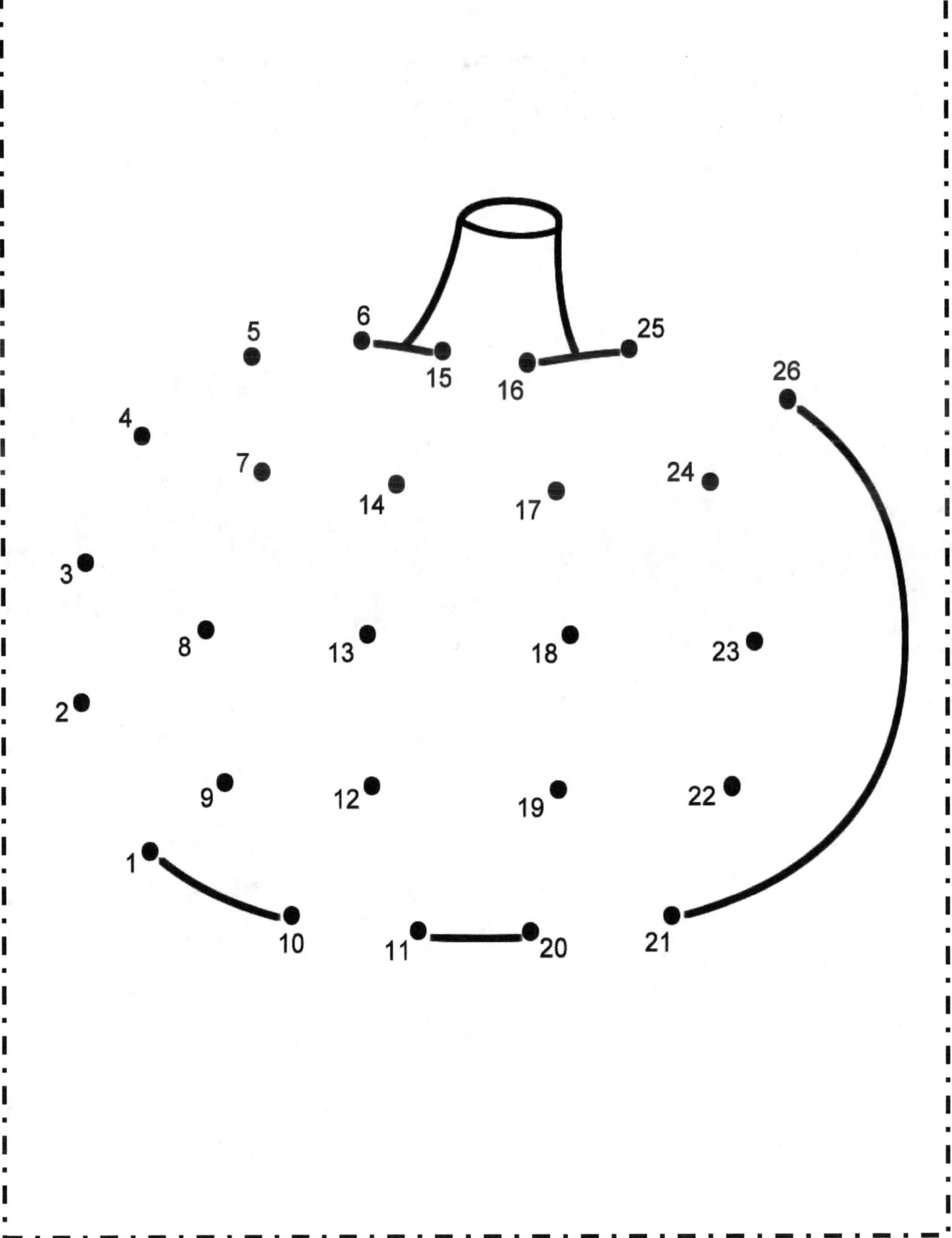
1
2
3
4
5
6
7
8
9
10
11
12
13
14
15
16
17
18
19
20
21
22
23
24
25
26

- "Why shouldn't you sit next to a turkey at dinner?
- "Because he will gobble it up."

FEEL FREE TO DRAW AND
COLOR ANYTHING YOU WANT

Save the Turkey Maze

Help Tom Turkey escape to freedom!

- "What do you call a running turkey?"
- "Fast Food."

Feel free to draw and color anything you want

Turkey Dot to Dot

FEEL FREE TO DRAW AND
COLOR ANYTHING YOU WANT

Save the Turkey Maze

Help Tom Turkey escape to freedom!

Feel free to draw and
color anything you want

- "What's the best song to play while cooking a turkey?"
- "All about that baste."

Save the Turkey Maze

Help Tom Turkey
escape to freedom!

FEEL FREE TO DRAW AND COLOR ANYTHING YOU WANT

Feel free to draw and color anything you want

- "Why did the turkey cross the road?"
- "He wanted people to think he was a chicken."

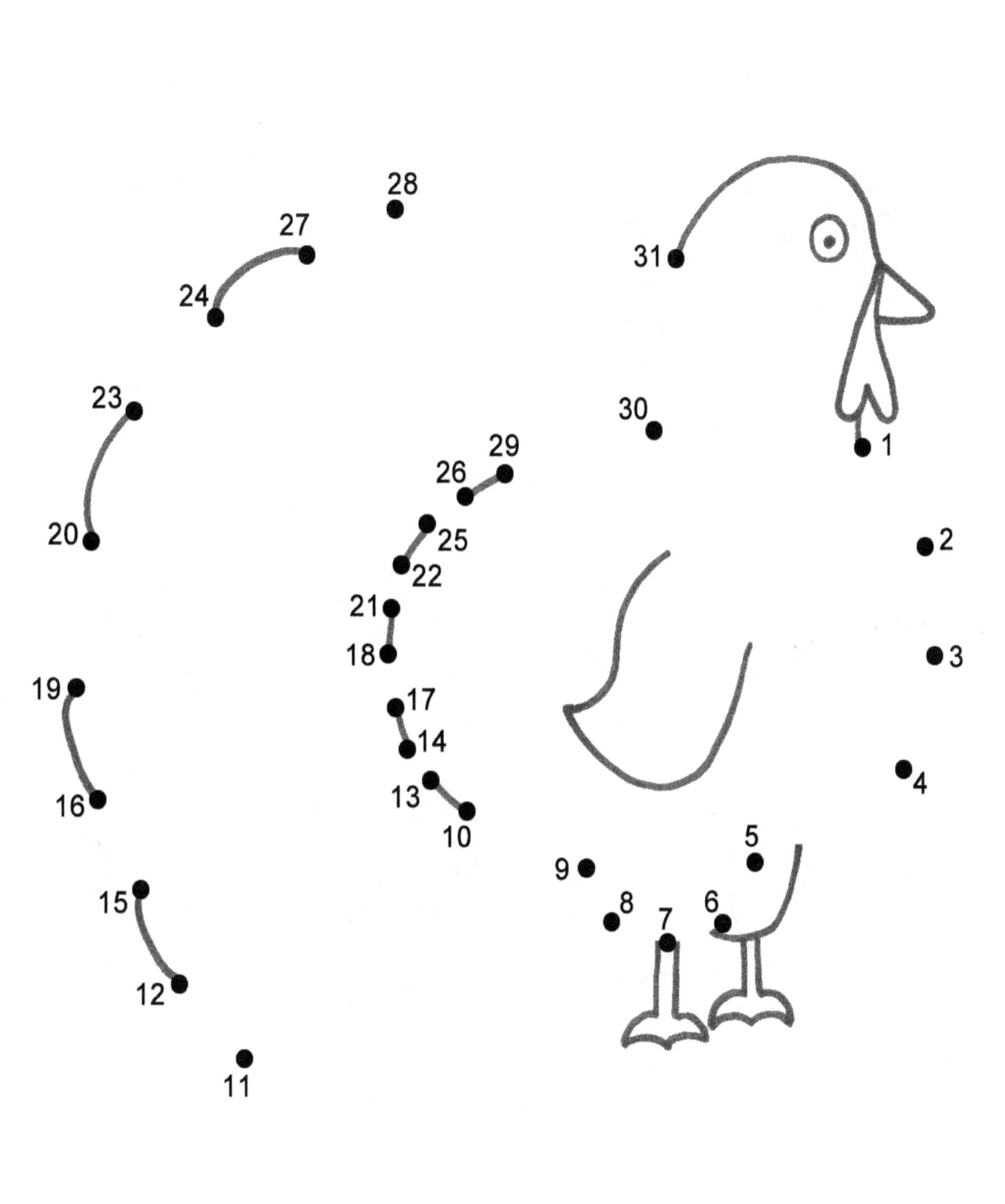

1
2
3
4
5
6
7
8
9
10
11
12
13
14
15
16
17
18
19
20
21
22
23
24
25
26
27
28
29
30
31

FEEL FREE TO DRAW AND
COLOR ANYTHING YOU WANT

FEEL FREE TO DRAW AND
COLOR ANYTHING YOU WANT

- "What did the turkey say to the computer?"
- "Google, google."

Feel free to draw and color anything you want

Feel free to draw and
color anything you want

FEEL FREE TO DRAW AND COLOR ANYTHING YOU WANT

- "What kind of weather does a turkey like?"
- "Fowl weather."

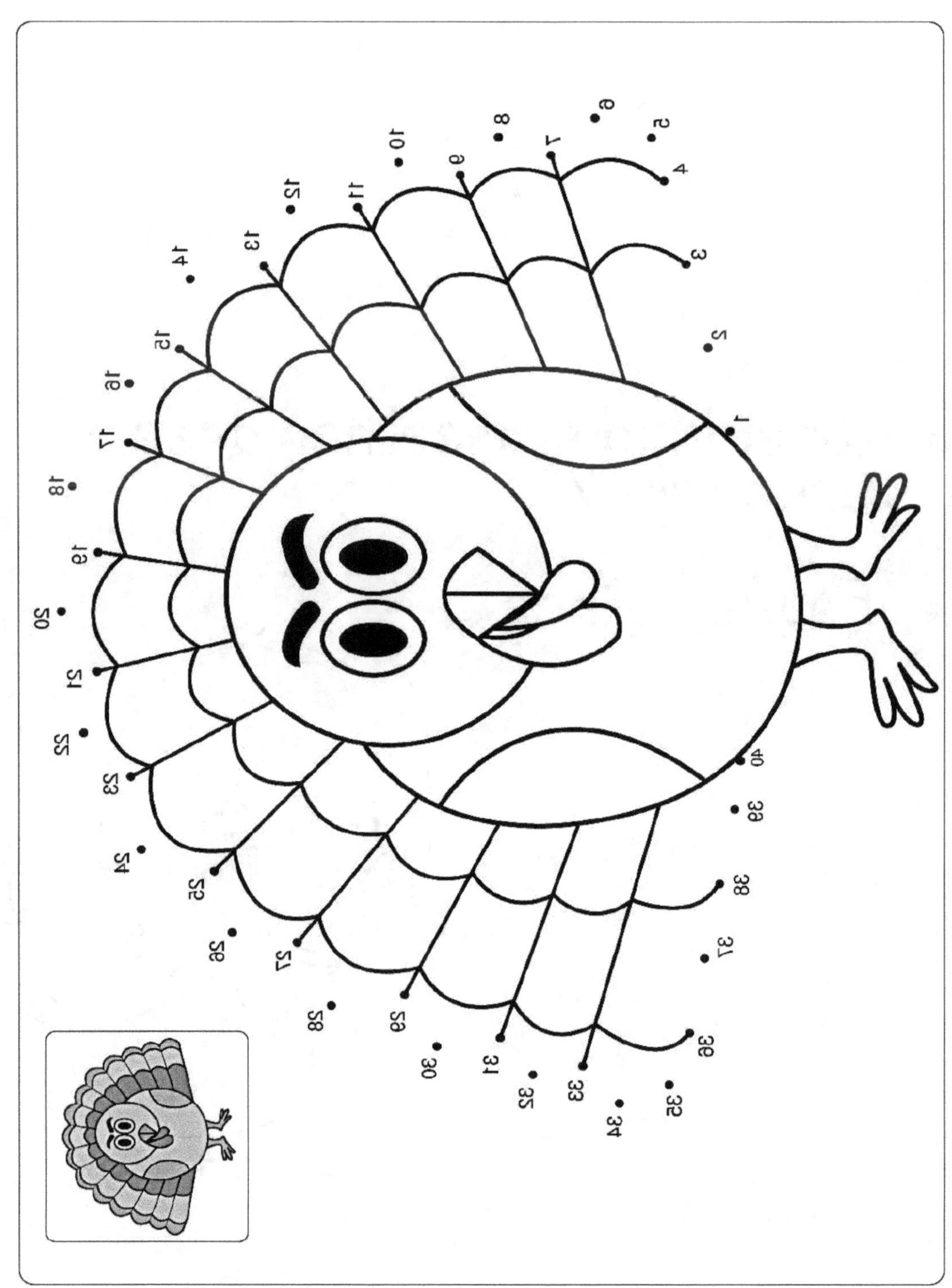

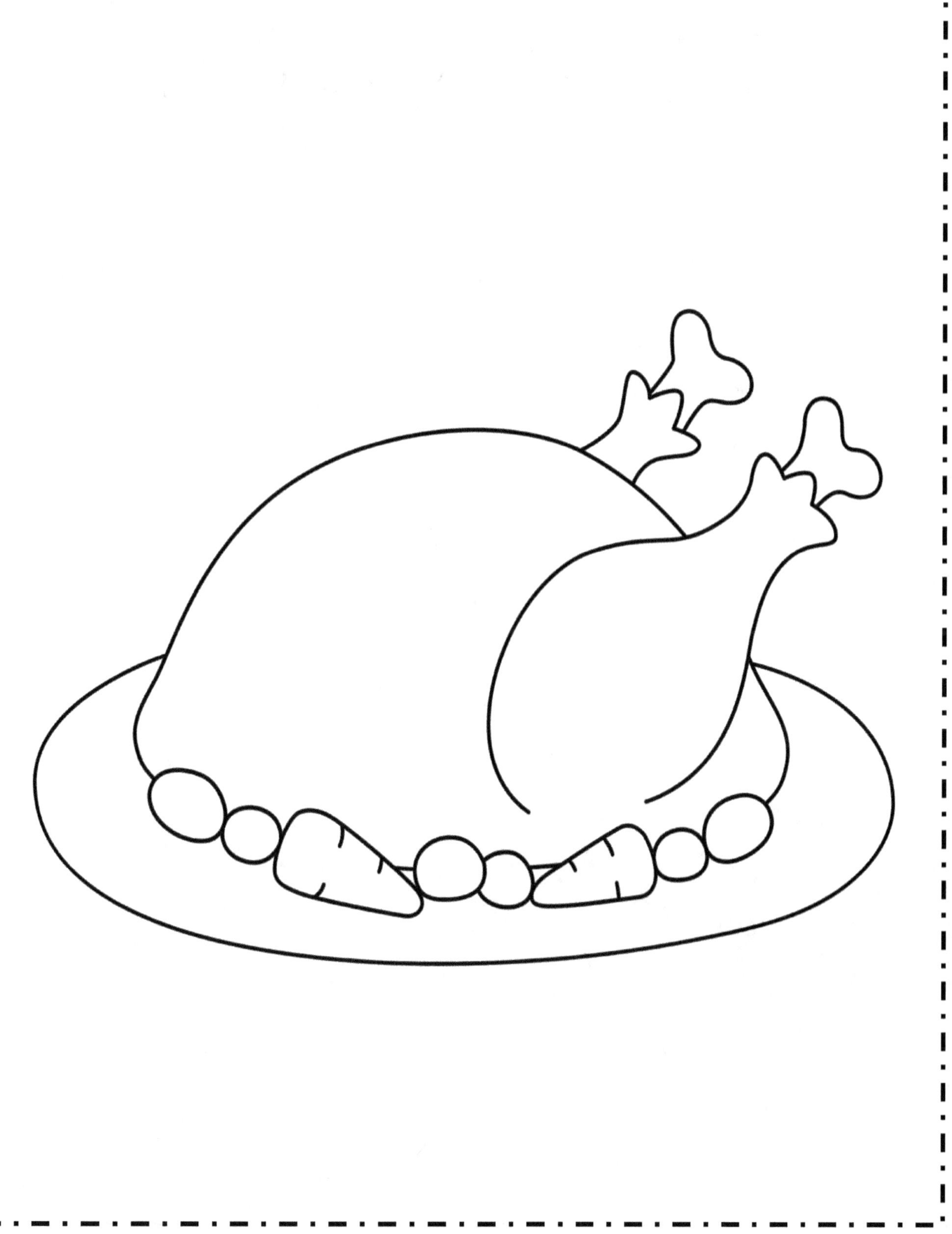

Feel free to draw and color anything you want

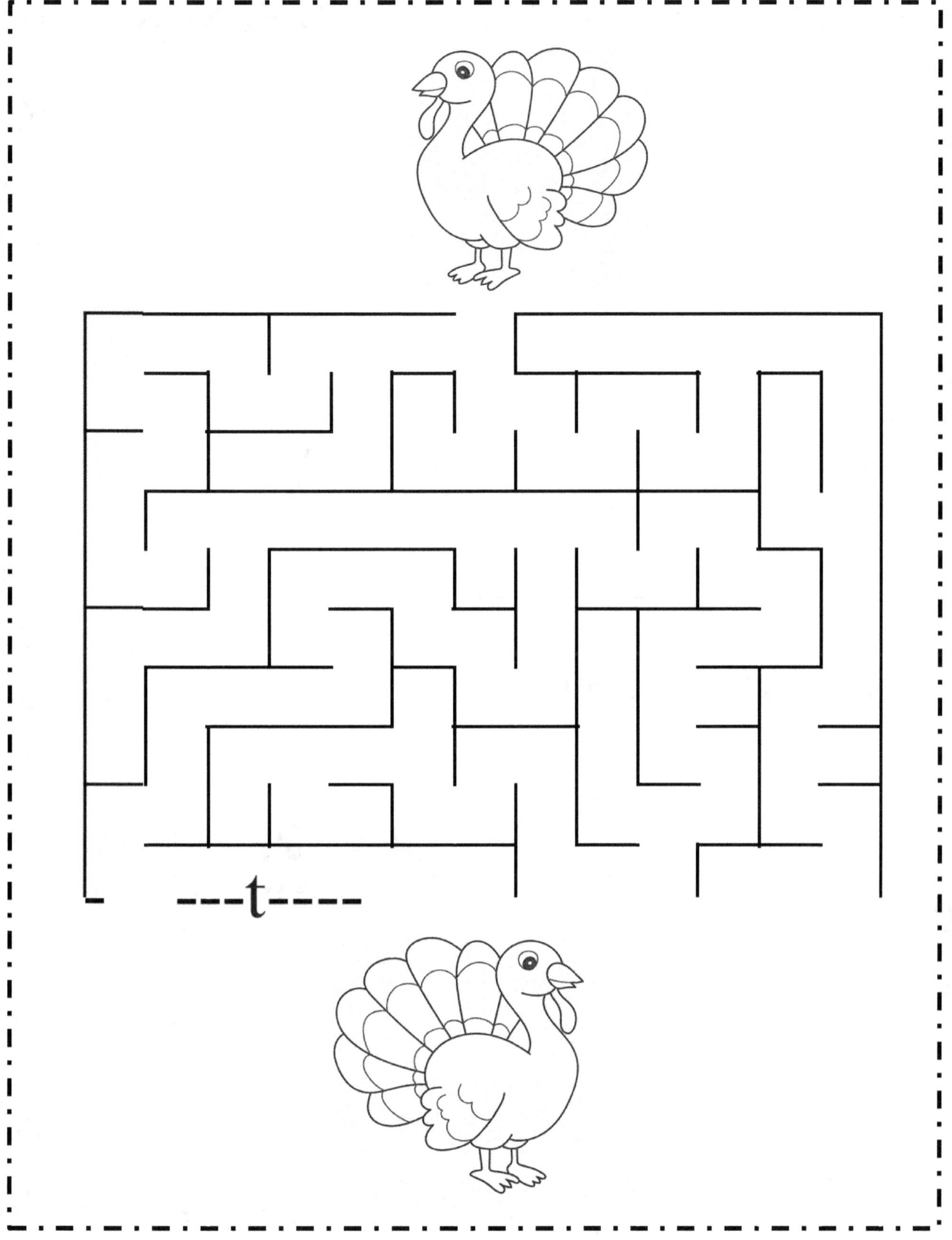
---t----

- What did the turkey say to the turkey hunter on Thanksgiving Day?

- Quack, Quack!

I am THANKFUL FOR :

blessed
grateful
thankful

www.ingramcontent.com/pod-product-compliance
Lightning Source LLC
LaVergne TN
LVHW080818170826
845678LV00011B/2064